P9-DGV-890

PART ONE

CHAPTER ONE

"**G**uys, check out my new guitar!" Kevin Lucas called to his brothers Nick and Joe as they entered the bedroom they all shared.

"Bedroom" didn't really do the space justice. Because this wasn't just a huge, supercool bedroom. Nor was it just the boy's favorite spot to hang out and chill. And it wasn't even merely the second-floor loft of the converted old firehouse in New Jersey where their whole family lived.

No, the loft was also the unofficial headquarters of the Lucas brothers' hugely popular band, JONAS. The place included a full recording studio, several keyboards, a bunch of amps and speakers, and tons of other world-famous-rock-band-type equipment, not to mention bunk beds made to look exactly like the ones on their tour bus, which they used when they wanted to feel as if they were back on the road. They had regular beds for sleeping, of course.

Given all that, it wasn't unusual to walk in and see Kevin plugging an electric guitar into an amplifier. After all, he *was* a rock star and he *was* obsessed with guitars. He had hundreds of them stored on a revolving rack in the back part of the loft. When JONAS was touring, they needed an extra bus just for Kevin's guitars.

What *was* unusual was this particular guitar. Its neck was about three times the length of a normal one. If a normal guitar was a duck, this guitar was an ostrich. A really, really tall ostrich with an extralong neck.

"I had it custom-made," Kevin said proudly when his brothers had seen the guitar.

Nick, the youngest—and usually most thoughtful—of the three, glanced at Joe. "That explains the fourteen-foot guitar case I just tripped over."

Kevin barely listened. He was too busy feeling the power surge through the guitar. It was a thing of true beauty.

"Dig it," he told his younger brothers eagerly. "On a normal guitar, this is the highest note you can hit, right?"

He played a short, rockin' lick. The guitar shredded and wailed awesomely. The sound bounced off the walls of the firehouse. Nick and Joe shrugged. Kevin's guitar sounded like, well, a guitar.

"But on the *Kevin-ated* guitar," Kevin went on as the echoes faded, "I can play way up *here*."

This time he started the same way. But when the guitar wailed out that high note, he kept going. Higher and higher. And then higher still.

Kevin just kept on shredding, working his way up the long, long, looooong neck.

Joe and Nick winced at the piercing sounds shrieking out of the guitar. Just when they thought they couldn't stand it any longer, the sounds stopped. Whew!

But when they looked at Kevin, he was still playing.

Joe was confused. "You look cool, but I don't hear anything."

"That's because the notes I'm playing are so high, humans can barely hear them," Kevin explained as he kept right on shredding. "Dogs can totally hear it, though."

Nick and Joe nodded. Now that he mentioned it, they could hear something still coming out of the amp. Just barely, though.

And still Kevin kept going. Higher, higher, high—

ZOMP!

There was a brief buzz, and then nothing. All the sound had stopped. Kevin felt the power drain out of his guitar and guessed that the electric cable had been yanked out of the wall. But who had done it? Nick and Joe were still standing right there in front of him.

Kevin glanced over at the wall and his eyes grew wide. A small dog was standing by the outlet. It had the cable in its mouth and a disgruntled expression on its face. All three Lucas brothers stared at the dog. It glared back. Then it dropped the cable on the floor, let out a low growl, and marched out of the room.

Kevin shrugged. "I said dogs could hear it. I didn't say dogs would like it."

"Whose dog was that, anyway?" Nick wondered.

Joe was peering out the way the dog had gone. "I don't know," he said. "But he left a review of Kevin's guitar in the corner." *And it looks like he's not a fan,* Joe added silently.

CHAPTER TWO

Kevin and Joe were so used to being onstage together that they often moved as one, even in their everyday life. On this particular morning, for example, they stepped forward, stopped, and turned. They wriggled their fingers in time to a silent beat. Then . . .

Clang!

As if by magic, their lockers swung open. It was just another day at their school, the Horace

Mantis Academy. Even though they had gotten pretty famous, their parents wanted them to stay grounded. Hence, regular high school. Quickly, Kevin and Joe began digging out their books for morning classes.

Ready to go, Kevin stepped back and looked around. The school hallways were crowded, as usual. Students were rushing around saying hi to their friends and getting ready for the day, as usual. Stella Malone was walking toward them looking stylish, as usu— Hang on. What the heck was Stella wearing?!

Kevin squeezed his eyes shut, wondering if they had suddenly gone wonky on him. It felt sort of like that time the TV had kept switching randomly between a test pattern and a Mexican *telenovela*. That had made his head hurt and his eyes cross in the same way this vision just had. Only this wasn't TV. This was real life.

When he opened his eyes again, nothing had changed. Stella was still coming toward him and Joe. And she was still wearing the most hideous, ridiculous-looking sweater Kevin had ever seen.

This was downright mind-boggling. Stella was a lifelong friend of the Lucas brothers and also served as JONAS's fashion stylist. She made sure that the band looked superhot and cutting-edge whenever they took the stage, posed for a photo, or even just walked down the street. In fact, at that very moment, Kevin and his brothers had Stella to thank for putting together the awesome outfits they were wearing.

Noticing his brother's confused expression, Joe also turned. "Hey, there's Stella," he said. Then he, too, did a double take. "Whoa, look at that sweater."

"Uh-oh," Kevin groaned. "She's going to ask us what we think of it. What do we say?"

Joe grinned. "So many bad sweater jokes, so little time!"

Kevin clutched at him in a panic. "You know I can't tell someone the truth if it might hurt their feelings!"

"Yeah." Joe rolled his eyes. He knew *exactly*

how his brother was when he lied. "You get all nervous, and your voice gets real high." He switched to a goofy falsetto to imitate Kevin. "What's up with that?"

Kevin bit his lip. "I guess it all started that one time when I had to tell that one girl the truth about that one thing. . . ."

He couldn't go on. Even the memory was painful. He needed a distraction. Quickly, he grabbed an acoustic guitar out of his locker. Kevin took a deep breath.

"Dude," Joe broke in before Kevin could do more than strum a couple of chords. "We don't have time for a song."

Kevin blinked. Maybe Joe was right. He put down the guitar.

"Anyway," Joe went on, "maybe she won't ask about the sweater."

At that very moment, Stella arrived in front of them. "Hey, guys," she said. "What do you think of my sweater?"

When he answered, Kevin's voice came out all

high and squeaky, just as he had feared it would. "That has got to be the most beautiful sweater I've ever seen in my life!"

"Thanks!" Stella smiled, oblivious to Kevin's lie. She turned. "Joe?"

"Stella, you know I love you," Joe said. "But that sweater looks like a peacock threw up on it."

Stella frowned. "This happens to be designed by Jacques Petite," she informed him, lovingly stroking the sweater's hideous multicolored sleeve. "He's the most cutting-edge designer coming out of France. Plus, it's completely biodegradable."

"Great," Joe said. "You won't have to feel guilty when you throw it in the trash."

Stella rolled her eyes. "Oh, what do you know?" she huffed.

"You two sound like an old married couple," Kevin observed.

"Old?!" Stella and Joe exclaimed at once, ignoring the "married" and "couple" parts.

Just then Nick hurried toward them, cutting off any additional protests. "Dudes, I've got some bad news," he said, panting. He caught sight of their stylist. "And it has nothing to do with Stella's horrible sweater."

Stella scowled at him, looking insulted. But Nick didn't even notice.

"Margot canceled," he went on, his expression serious. "She can't record with us tomorrow night."

"What?" Kevin cried. "She's my favorite backup singer!"

"She has a frog in her throat," Nick explained.

Kevin nodded. At least half of his biology class had spent yesterday's lab time hacking and wheezing. "Yeah, there's some kind of bug going around," he said.

Nick shook his head. "No," he corrected. "She was swimming in a swamp and got an actual *frog* in her throat. She's at the clinic now getting a frog-ectomy."

Kevin was surprised to hear that. He hadn't even known people went swimming in swamps.

And even if they did, what had Margot been doing swimming in one two days before a recording session? And where had she even *found* a swamp, anyway? As far as he knew, there were no swamps nearby.

Then again, he was no swamp expert. Besides, all that was beside the point. The point was . . . what was the point? Right! They were down one awesome backup singer.

By now Joe looked just as anxious as Nick. He ran a hand through his dark, perfectly-styled hair. "What are we going to do?" he exclaimed. "Malcolm Meckle is coming to watch us lay down tracks."

"Malcolm Meckle?" Kevin blurted out. "The president of our record label?"

Nick nodded. "So we need to find a replacement female backup singer. Fast."

He didn't get to say more because . . . *THWOCK!* A football came out of nowhere and nailed Joe right in the head. He dropped like a stone.

CHAPTER THREE

Kevin and Nick shook their heads. Had that actually just happened? They stared down at their brother, who was lying on the ground. Apparently it had.

A moment later Joe struggled to his feet, wincing as the world spun around him.

"Sorry, sorry, sorry!" A breathless voice came from behind them.

Turning, the brothers saw Macy Misa rushing

toward them. She was wearing a football uniform, complete with helmet, pads, and cleats.

Macy was Stella's best friend. She had two great passions in life—sports and JONAS. She was great at one and a bit of a mess at the other. Macy could stare down any opponent on a softball field, tennis court, or bowling lane with steely determination. But one glimpse of the Lucas brothers and that stare went all gooey and soft around the edges, trimmed in pink lace and little hand-drawn hearts.

"I'm so sorry," she blurted out as she skidded to a stop in front of her idols and picked up the football. "I was just working on a new throw. See, it starts here—"

She swung her hand back to demonstrate. *THWACK!* She smacked Nick upside the head.

"*Aargh!*" Nick shouted.

"Sorry!" Macy cried.

She couldn't believe she'd nearly taken out another of her favorite superstars. She swung around to make sure she wouldn't accidentally spaz out and hit him again.

KONK!

"Yowwww!" yelped Joe.

"Sorry!" Macy exclaimed again. She spun around.

"Ow!" Kevin howled as she stomped right on his foot.

"Sorry!"

Stella had seen enough of the carnage. It was time to step in. She hurried forward, placing herself between Macy and the guys.

"Macy, remember the drill," she ordered. "Deep breaths."

Macy heaved in a huge breath. Then another. Breathe in, breathe out. Just like Stella had taught her.

"I don't get it," Stella said as she watched her friend try to get control of herself. "You're this amazing, graceful athlete, but anytime you're around JONAS you become a hallway hazard."

Macy couldn't help being a little insulted. A

hallway hazard? That was carrying things a little too far, wasn't it?

"I have no idea what you're talking about." Macy turned toward Stella. The boys ducked out of the way—just in case.

Stella glanced at them. "Let's get you guys some ice," she told Joe and Nick. Then she turned to Kevin. "How are your toes?"

Kevin glanced down, wriggling his foot inside his shoe. "Three okay, two iffy," he reported. "But I'm good."

Stella nodded, then led Nick and Joe away. Both of them clutched their heads as they followed her.

"Don't forget to ask about a new backup singer!" Kevin called after them.

Macy's eyes lit up. "You need a new backup singer?" she exclaimed.

Kevin gulped. He was now alone with Destructo Girl. He kept a wary eye on her as she advanced toward him.

"You know, *I'm* a singer," Macy said excitedly.

"In fact, it's always been a dream of mine to turn pro. But, you know, I'm so busy with all the sports. . . ."

She raised the football to illustrate her point. Kevin lunged for it before it could attack one of his body parts.

With the ball safely in his own hands, Kevin could turn his attention back to Macy. And also to what she'd just said. So, a wanting-to-turn-pro singer? Standing right here in the school hallway in front of him? Right when JONAS needed a new backup singer? What were the odds? It was almost as wild as having three brothers who all loved to sing and could play . . . Hey, wait a minute, Kevin thought. I guess it's not *that* crazy.

"If it's always been your dream, then you should follow your heart," he told her. "Why don't you come sing backup on our new song tomorrow?"

"Oh, my gosh!" Macy blurted out. "Really? Is this really happening? You can't be serious!"

She felt light-headed, as if little stars were

bursting inside her brain. Stars of bliss and perfection. So many stars that they crowded out the rest of her brain, and she fainted.

A second later, she popped back up. "But you are!" she cried incoherently.

She was already picturing the amazing scene. Her, Macy Misa, singing in a real studio. With JONAS! What could be better than that?

Then another thought occurred to her. "What if I'm not good enough?" she asked, her forehead creasing with worry.

Kevin shrugged. "No sweat. I'll give you a few pointers before we record."

"Thank you, thank you, thank you!" Macy shrieked, jumping up and down. Unfortunately, on one of the "downs" she landed on something soft and sort of crunchy. Namely, Kevin's foot.

"*Aaaargh!*" Kevin cried.

Macy stopped jumping. "I'm so sorry!" she exclaimed.

"No problem." Kevin grimaced, hoping that feeling would return to his foot soon. "They say, technically, you don't need your pinky toe," he added.

He hobbled off down the hall. Aside from his throbbing foot, he was feeling pretty good. Nick and Joe were going to be psyched when they heard about this. Well, not the crushed-foot part. But the other part—the part where he'd found them a new backup singer and saved the day.

Kevin grinned. Sometimes even *he* had to wonder exactly how he'd turned out so incredibly awesome.

CHAPTER FOUR

Tom Lucas was downstairs in the firehouse. As the father of three teenage boys and a younger son all-too-eager to be a teenager, he stayed pretty busy. Being JONAS's manager kept him even busier.

Today Mr. Lucas's job was to look through some prototypes of JONAS merchandise. The stuff filled the table in front of him. Clothes. Posters. Toys. And more. Mr. Lucas was supposed to decide which items they should put into production to sell at JONAS concerts and on their Web site.

He picked up one of the items. It was a boomerang with the band's logo on it.

"Ooh," he said, intrigued. "A JONAS boomerang!"

He decided to test it out. Winding up, he flung it away as hard as he could. Then he waited for it to come back.

And waited.

And waited some more.

Finally he gave up. Picking up a note card, Mr. Lucas jotted a few words on it.

"Boomerang not boomerang-y," he muttered as he wrote.

Hearing something, he looked up, ready to catch the flying object. But it wasn't the boomerang. It was his youngest son, Frankie. Frankie was not only the youngest Lucas brother, he was also JONAS's unofficial mascot.

"Hey, Frankie," Mr. Lucas greeted him. He

gestured at the table. "Just checking out new merchandise for the next tour. Manager types like myself call it 'merch.' I'm on a 'merch search.'"

He chuckled at his own joke. Frankie just stared at him, unamused.

Mr. Lucas cleared his throat. "Yeah. Anyway . . ." Holding up a bag of something dry and leathery, he squinted at the label. "'JONAS Jerky'?" he read aloud. "'All the rock-and-roll goodness of JONAS in salted and cured beef.'" He glanced at Frankie again. "What do you think?"

Frankie didn't hesitate. "I think you need this new T-shirt," he said, holding up a shirt. A huge picture covered almost all of it. A picture of Frankie. As if it weren't clear enough, the name FRANKIE was spelled out above the picture in huge letters.

Mr. Lucas examined it. "Let's see," he said. "Nice picture of you. Doesn't have the name of the band . . . or any members of the band . . . or say anything about the band . . ." He shrugged. "I'm going to have to say no."

Frankie scowled. "This isn't over!" he snapped. He grabbed back the T-shirt and took off. Mr. Lucas sighed as he watched him go.

CLONK! Just then something bonked him on the head and fell to the floor.

It was the boomerang. Mr. Lucas glanced at it, rubbed his head, and reached for his note card again.

"*Too* boomerang-y," he muttered as he wrote.

CHAPTER FIVE

Meanwhile, back at Horace Mantis, it was lunchtime. Nick, Joe, and Stella were sitting together. The brothers were having the cafeteria's daily special—sloppy joes, with an emphasis on the sloppy.

"How can you guys eat sloppy joes?" Stella asked as she watched Nick lift the sandwich up to his mouth, the contents oozing precariously. "I custom-made those outfits. Do you realize how much the shirts cost?"

Joe shrugged, unconcerned. Then he took a bite of his sloppy joe. As his teeth bit down on the front half, the back half slid out of the bun and landed in his lap. Oops.

Stella grimaced.

"What?" Joe protested. "I completely missed the shirt!"

Before Stella could argue that the pants weren't any cheaper, Kevin walked up and sat down with them. He didn't seem to notice the mess. Or the annoyed look on Stella's face. Actually, he looked kind of distracted. And sort of excited. That worried Joe and Nick. A distracted, excited Kevin was rarely good news. At least for anyone besides Kevin.

"Hey, guys," Kevin said, sounding as distracted and excited as he looked. "I told Macy she could sing backup on our new song."

Stella had just taken a sip of her drink. At Kevin's words, she spit it back out again. All over Joe's blazer.

"What?!" she shrieked. Noticing Joe staring down at his blazer, she shrugged. "I'll get that out with seltzer." Then she turned her full attention back to Kevin. "How could you do that?"

Stella's reaction surprised Kevin. Okay, so Stella could get a little worked up about things sometimes. Like that mess of tomato sauce and ground something-or-other in Joe's lap, for instance. Even Kevin could see that that couldn't be good for a guy's superstylish pants. But what was there to get so upset over about what *he'd* just said? Macy was one of Stella's best friends. She should be happy for her!

"Why not?" he asked. "We're going to make her dream come true. And I think it will be cool to have a fan sing on our record."

Nick and Joe nodded. "Totally," one of them said.

"Way cool," the other added.

But Stella couldn't have told you which Lucas brother had said what. She was far too focused on Kevin—and the huge mistake he was about to make. The absolute chaos and utter destruction he was about to unleash on JONAS. Possibly the world. And she *wasn't* being overly dramatic.

"Listen," she said urgently. "Macy's my best friend. But the girl is a *terrible* singer. Terrible with a capital *Whoa*."

"She told me she was pretty good," Kevin said, beginning to look worried. "She's thought about going pro."

Nick glanced at Stella. "If she's that bad, why haven't you told her?" It was bound to have come up in the past, and Stella usually had no problem being honest.

"It would crush her," Stella pointed out, biting her lower lip anxiously. "She's way sensitive and delicate."

As if on cue, Macy herself appeared. She was walking through the cafeteria with another athlete. For once, she didn't notice that all three members of her favorite band were there—*and* watching her intently.

"Oh, yeah, jerk-face?" she taunted the other

athlete. "When I see you on the ice, I'm gonna body-slam you into tomorrow and use your lopsided head as a hockey puck!"

She passed out of view, still trash-talking for all she was worth. Nick nodded appreciatively.

"Good lungs," he said. "And if she can carry a tune, Kevin can help her sound awesome."

Kevin had to agree with that. He was awesome at helping people sound awesome. "How bad can she be?" he asked.

Stella stared at him grimly. They weren't getting it. "One time during a softball game, she was singing 'Take Me Out to the Ballgame,' and they called animal control because they thought there was an injured manatee on the field." She paused to let that sink in. "A *manatee*!" she repeated for emphasis. They lived in oceans. And were silent . . . usually—unless, apparently, they weren't.

The three brothers exchanged concerned looks. Joe and Nick were wondering if Kevin had made a terrible mistake. Kevin was wondering how the manatee Stella mentioned had been injured, and if it was all right now.

One thing was for sure—they had a potential crisis to fix.

CHAPTER SIX

After school that day, Kevin waited for Macy in the school's atrium. Since he had gotten the band into this mess, Joe and Nick had decided that he would be the one to find out just how messy the mess would be. Just then, Kevin spotted Macy hurrying toward him. She was carrying something in a sort of cloth sling. When she got closer, he saw that it was a bowling ball. This was not good. . . .

"Sorry I'm late," Macy greeted him breathlessly. "I had bowling prac—"

"*Aargh!*" Kevin yowled as the bowling ball slipped out of its carrier—and landed right on his foot.

"I'm so sorry!" Macy cried. "Did I hurt your foot?"

"I'm not sure." Kevin flexed his toes. Or what he suspected might be his toes. "I can't tell where the pain from before ends and where the new pain begins."

"I'm just so nervous," Macy explained, looking sheepish.

She remembered what Stella told her to do when she was having a JONAS attack. Deep breaths, Stella always said. So Macy breathed in. Out. In again. Out . . . There, that was better. A little.

"I can't believe an actual member of JONAS is going to help me with my singing," she said when she was calmer. "Thank you so much!"

"It's all good," Kevin said. "Why don't we

get started by singing some simple scales?"

"Sure, great." Macy took another deep breath. This time she let it out in the first note of a scale. . . .

Kevin wasn't sure what happened. One second he was standing there waiting for Macy to start singing. The next everything had gone black.

"Kevin," Macy's anxious voice floated into the blackness. "Kevin?"

Slowly, Kevin returned to consciousness. He opened his eyes and saw Macy's worried face staring down at him.

"Kevin," the face said, "are you okay?"

Kevin realized he was lying on the ground in the atrium. He pushed himself up. "Wh-what happened?" he stammered. "The last thing I heard was an injured manatee."

"I don't know," Macy said. "I started singing, and you fainted."

Kevin slowly climbed to his feet. Whew, that had been really weird. He didn't usually go around fainting like that. Maybe there'd been something strange in his food. You never really knew with sloppy joes. Or maybe his toes were more sensitive than he knew.

In any case, there was no time to worry about it now. Not if he wanted to have Macy ready to go in time for that recording session.

"Why don't we try again?" he said.

Macy nodded. Then she took another deep breath and started to sing.

At least that was what Kevin guessed she was trying to do. Her mouth was open, and sound was coming out. Horrible, horrible sound. Painful, inhuman, mind-numbing, injured-manatee–like sound . . .

He felt himself start to wobble. His vision started to go cloudy and stars swam before his eyes. Luckily, this time he managed to grab hold of a handy tree in time to steady himself. He could do it. He could survive this. . . .

Macy's face squinched up as she went for

a high note. Her voice warbled as she hit it and held it. Kevin felt himself shaking harder. The tree he was holding onto was shaking, too. Leaves scattered around him. Flowers wilted. Finally, a stunned seagull thudded to the ground and lay there gasping.

"*Aaaaaaaaaaah!*" Macy sang. Then she stopped and looked hopefully over at Kevin. "Well?" she asked.

Kevin shook his head. How was he going to break this to her? Stella had been right. Macy couldn't sing. She *shouldn't* sing. It wasn't healthy for him. Or anyone else.

He watched as the stunned seagull staggered to its feet, flapped its wings, and flew away. Then Kevin cleared his throat.

"I have to be honest with you," he told Macy. "Your singing is . . . You sounded like . . ."

Macy gazed up at him, waiting. She looked so sweet now that the horrible noises had stopped. So trusting and vulnerable . . . with her big, kind eyes . . .

Kevin sighed. He just couldn't do it. It would be like kicking a kitten.

"You sounded beautiful," he said, his voice almost as high-pitched as Macy's high note. Inwardly he groaned. He was such a bad liar.

Macy didn't seem to notice. "Really?" she cried happily.

Kevin's voice got even higher. "Really. *Really* good."

"You're not just saying that?" Macy asked, a huge smile spreading over her face.

"No." By this time, Kevin's voice was reaching dog-irritating heights. "You sounded great!"

"Wow!" Macy clasped her hands blissfully. "If an honest, attractive, professional JONAS like you tells me I'm great, then . . . I must be great! I'm giving up all my sports and devoting all my time to singing!"

Kevin smiled weakly. *What had he done?*

"Look out, world!" Macy cried, spreading her arms. "Here comes Macy Misa, singer extraordinaire!" Then she took a deep breath and belted out a note. *"Aaaaaaaaah!"*

Kevin heard the atrium's glass windows crack. "Great!" he screeched in his highest-pitched voice yet. "Really great!"

CHAPTER SEVEN

When Kevin returned home and went up to the loft, he found Nick, Joe, and Stella waiting for him. Stella was still wearing her awful sweater. That didn't seem quite fair to Kevin. After having his ears assaulted by Macy's singing, did he really have to have his eyes assaulted, too? And in his own room?

"So?" Stella asked, looking very curious. "How'd the music lesson go?"

Kevin did his best to avert his eyes from what he now thought of as The Sweater. "Great," he squeaked out in his high-pitched "liar" voice. Then he cleared his throat. "Good," he added, his voice still pretty high. He tried one more time. "It was awful!" This time his voice came out nice and normal. "I wanted to be honest with Macy, but I just couldn't."

"I don't know what your problem is," Joe told him. He *never* had a problem telling people what they needed to hear. "You just have to phrase it right."

Kevin frowned. "She might be the worst singer ever singing in the history of awful singers singing. How can that be 'phrased right'?" He put his curly-haired head in his hands.

Joe shrugged. "What you just said sounded pretty good."

Nick was looking thoughtful—as usual. "If Macy wants to sing professionally, she's going to have to get used to criticism," he pointed out in his most logical, Nick-like way. "Even if it means being brutally honest."

"You're right." Kevin nodded. "Macy has to be told the horrible, soul-shattering truth." He glanced over at Stella. "Man, I'd hate to be in your shoes." The bad news, in his opinion, would be easier to take coming from a friend.

"Oh, no!" Stella retorted. "This isn't *my* problem. This is *your* problem."

Nick shook his head. There was more at stake here than feelings. "We can't risk having her sing in front of Malcolm Meckle," Nick pointed out. "This is the first time he's going to hear our new songs."

"We want to impress him, not melt his brain," Joe added.

Kevin sighed. "I just can't tell someone the truth if it's going to hurt their feelings." He nodded toward Stella. "It'd be like me telling you that's a really ugly sweater." Realizing what he'd just done, he gulped. "Which it's not," he added quickly. "But if it *were* ugly, I wouldn't say it. But it's not. But if—"

"Stop talking!" Nick ordered him.

"I've got to tell Macy the truth," Kevin said, yanking himself back on track.

"We'll go with you for support," Joe offered.

Nick nodded. "You're going to need it."

Downstairs, unaware of his eldest son's dilemma, Mr. Lucas was reading some band-related paperwork. He lowered it to find Frankie standing there staring at him.

"Whoa!" Mr. Lucas jumped, startled. "You're a sneaky little one, aren't you?"

Frankie held up his latest T-shirt design. This time there was a slightly smaller picture of him on it, along with a really, really small picture of his brothers. And this time the word JONAS was just as big as the word FRANKIE.

"Happy?" Frankie asked his father.

Mr. Lucas squinted at the shirt. "Is that supposed to be your brothers?" he asked. "You can barely see them."

"That's why it comes with this." Frankie held

up a magnifying glass. Added value was always a big draw.

Mr. Lucas shook his head. "Try again."

Frankie scowled. Then he tucked the shirt and magnifying glass under his arm and stomped out of the room.

Mr. Lucas picked up his paperwork again, smiling at his youngest son's antics. "Keeps him busy, anyway," he murmured as he went back to work.

CHAPTER EIGHT

The next day at school, the first thing Kevin did was go in search of Macy. It was time to break the news. Joe and Nick were with him for backup. They soon spotted Macy at her locker. She was holding a bunch of books . . . and a field-hockey stick.

Standing a safe distance away, Kevin's brothers tried to psych him up for the task ahead. "Okay, champ," Joe said in his peppiest pep-talk voice.

"There's Macy. Go tell her the truth. You can do it."

Nick rubbed Kevin's shoulders like a trainer getting ready to send his star boxer into the ring. "The truth will set us free," he said—"from her terrible singing."

Kevin nodded. He started to bob and weave, feeling loose. He even threw a few air punches.

"Gonna tell her the truth," he muttered fiercely. "Gonna set us free."

Joe grabbed a sponge and sponged off Kevin's forehead. "Eye of the tiger," he said. "Eye of the tiger!"

Then Nick held up a sports bottle. Kevin opened his mouth, and Nick squirted water into it. Joe held up a bucket for Kevin to spit into. They were nothing if not prepared.

Kevin was now totally psyched up. "Let's do this!" he grunted.

Before Kevin could change his mind, the three approached Macy. She was busy with the books she was holding and didn't see them coming.

"Hey, Macy," Kevin greeted her.

She spun around as if stung by a bee. All three brothers had to duck to avoid being struck by her field-hockey stick.

Kevin took a deep breath. Danger or not, there was no backing down now. No chickening out. "I kind of need to talk to you about your singing a little bit," he said.

Hmm. That had come out a little flatter—and less authoritative—than he had anticipated.

"My singing?" Macy asked, looking suddenly nervous.

Just then, one of her books slipped out of her grasp and hit the floor. As she bent over to retrieve it, Kevin, Joe, and Nick had to lean way back as the hockey stick whizzed by, barely missing them.

"Um," Kevin said, "the thing is . . ."

This had seemed so easy five minutes ago. Now he could tell he was losing it.

"Well," Kevin started again, "your singing. It's kind of . . . This thing is . . . You know what . . . Here's the thing . . ."

Macy looked at the other guys for translation.

"He loves the beginnings of sentences," Joe told her helpfully.

Suddenly Nick got a brainstorm. "What Kevin's trying to say is, are you still singing backup for us after school?"

Kevin and Joe turned and stared at their brother. What could have made Nick suddenly go insane? Macy hadn't even sung a note yet, so you couldn't blame it on that.

"Totally!" Macy told Nick happily.

"Cool." Nick smiled back at her. "See you there."

As Macy skipped off, looking excited, Joe continued to stare at his younger brother. "Nick," he said, "what happened to setting us free?"

"Yeah," Kevin put in. "I was just about to tell her the truth."

Nick rolled his eyes. "The only thing you were about to do was pass out. And it doesn't matter anyway, because I have an idea and it's foolproof."

Kevin straightened his shoulders. "That means

even *I* can't mess it up!" He smiled. That was always a good plan.

Nick explained his idea. "We let Macy record, but we don't use her voice on the song," he said. "She won't know the difference, so she won't get her feelings hurt."

"And what about Malcolm Meckle?" Kevin asked.

"Malcolm Meckle mustn't meet Macy Misa!" Nick declared. Then he grinned. "See what I did there? With all the *M*'s?"

Joe and Kevin sighed. "Yeah, yeah . . ."

"Anyway, we'll bring Macy in early," Nick went on. "She'll be gone before Malcolm even gets there."

Joe clapped him on the shoulder. "Bro, you are a genius!"

"Actually, three points shy of a genius." Nick shrugged modestly. "But who's counting?"

By later that afternoon, Frankie had another T-shirt ready. He pulled it on, paused just long enough to admire himself in the mirror, then went to show it to his father. This shirt consisted of a nice photo of all four brothers together and a caption reading TEAM JONAS.

"You know what?" Mr. Lucas said when he saw the design. "I like it! You've captured the family team spirit perfectly. Great job!"

Frankie looked down at the T-shirt. He could hardly believe his ears. After all the rejection, the humiliation, the petty criticism, was his genius finally going to be recognized?

"For real?" he demanded.

"So real, we have a deal," his father said.

Frankie held up a contract. "Sign here," he ordered. He had come prepared.

Mr. Lucas took the papers and smiled. "You're adorable!" he exclaimed. Then he signed on the dotted line.

"Aaaaaand here," Frankie said, pointing to another dotted line.

Mr. Lucas signed again. Suddenly a stuffy-looking man in a suit walked in. He looked over the contract, then stamped it repeatedly with an official-looking seal. Without a word, he turned and exited.

Mr. Lucas was a little startled. A notary? Where had Frankie found one on such short notice?

"Thank you, sir," he stammered. "I mean, Frankie."

Frankie grinned. Then he turned to exit with the contract tucked under his arm. Mr. Lucas was now staring off in the direction in which the notary had gone, so he didn't notice the back of Frankie's T-shirt.

That was probably just as well. The back of the shirt was completely taken up by a gigantic picture of Frankie's face.

CHAPTER NINE

Later that afternoon, the loft was prepped and ready for a serious recording session. The glassed-in, soundproof recording booth was lit up. The mixing board was humming. Nick and both his brothers were sitting at the board making last-minute adjustments.

"Okay, Macy," Nick said, pressing the TALK button on the mixing board. "We're about as ready as we're ever going to get out here."

Macy was inside the booth looking excited. "I can't believe I'm actually in the JONAS recording studio!" she squealed over the speaker.

"Neither can we," Joe muttered. Nick had stopped pressing the TALK button by now, which meant that Macy couldn't hear them from inside the booth. They could speak freely—and safely.

Nick glanced over at Kevin. "Run us through it one more time," he said. "She opens her mouth, and . . . ?"

"First you feel it more than hear it." Kevin shuddered as the memory overwhelmed him. The horrible, horrible memory. "Then there's a blinding white flash, which means you've got about ten seconds before you pass out."

"But no symptoms of vertigo or nausea?" Nick asked.

"Nope," Kevin replied. "I just got real dizzy and puked."

Nick stifled a groan. It wasn't worth explaining to Kevin that he had just defined vertigo and nausea. They didn't have the time. "Okay, let's do this."

The guys hit a few more buttons and adjusted a few more levels. Finally everything was perfect. Hitting one last button, an instrumental track began to play.

As the guys focused on the board, an imposing-looking man entered the loft. It was Malcolm Meckle, the record executive.

"Hey, there are my boys," Malcolm announced proudly, tapping his foot in time with the track. "Listen to that sound. *That's* what I'm talkin' about!"

The three brothers jumped in surprise and spun around.

"Malcolm Meckle!" Joe blurted out.

Nick looked nervous. And a little sick. "We weren't expecting you for another hour."

Just then, from inside the booth, Macy started to sing. If you could call it that.

All three brothers cringed. Malcolm flinched as if somebody had just punched him in the ear. Both ears. Really hard.

Joe knew they had to do something. Fast.

"So," he began, speaking as loudly as he could to cover the sound of Macy's "singing," "how was the traffic?"

Seeing what his brother was doing, Kevin did his best to help out. "Did you know the blue whale is the world's largest mammal?" he said conversationally.

But their distraction didn't work. Malcolm barely heard them. His ears were focused on the noise assaulting them.

"*What is that?*" he exclaimed. "That is *not* what I'm talkin' about!"

Malcolm's legs suddenly felt shaky. Too shaky to hold him up. He collapsed to his knees.

"Make it stop!" he wailed wretchedly. "Make it stop!"

Just then, a panicked-looking Mr. Lucas rushed in. "Everyone out of the building!" he shouted. "Sounds like a gas main just blew!"

Joe raised both hands. "Everybody calm

down!" he cried. "Just calm down!" Then he pushed the TALK button and spoke calmly into the mic. "That was great for us, Macy," he said. "Just a sec." Then he let the button go.

"Great?" Malcolm cried in disbelief. "Do you know what you're talkin' about? I don't think that's what you're talkin' about, 'cause that is *not* what I'm talkin' about!"

"Look," Nick said, "we know she sounds awful, but she's a friend and we said we'd let her record."

"We're never going to use this stuff on our CD," Joe added.

Malcolm hesitated. His ears were still ringing with that . . . that . . . Well, you certainly couldn't call it *singing*. . . .

"We've got to talk about this," he told the guys grimly.

Kevin hardly heard him. He'd just noticed where Joe was sitting. "Dude!" he cried in a panic, shoving him out of the way. "You're sitting on the TALK button. She can hear everything you're saying!"

Joe shook his head, glancing at the console. "No, I'm not," he said. "The button is over there."

He pointed to the actual TALK button. Kevin heaved a huge sigh of relief.

"Phew! That was close," he said. Then he turned back to the problem at hand. "So Macy isn't the greatest singer," he told Malcolm. "As soon as we finish the recording, we can erase her voice, and no one will ever have to hear her singing again. We just want to get through this without hurting her feelings."

While Kevin talked, an odd expression crept over his father's face. He was staring at something behind Kevin and the others.

"That's really considerate of you guys," he said, speaking up. "But she's standing right there."

Kevin and his brothers whirled around. Sure enough, Macy had stepped out of the soundproof recording booth while they weren't looking. Now she was right there, looking crushed.

Kevin held his breath. How much had she heard?

Macy burst into tears. Before anyone could say a word, she raced out of the room, sobbing loudly.

Apparently she'd heard enough.

CHAPTER TEN

The next morning Kevin stood at his locker at school pulling out greeting card after greeting card. His mother had taught him it was always best to be prepared. Nearby, his brothers stood waiting.

"'Happy Groundhog Day,'" Kevin muttered, tossing one card aside. "'Congratulations on Your New Nose.' 'Happy Belated Wednesday.'" He tossed those cards aside, too, and reached for another. Suddenly his expression brightened. "Hey, how about this one?"

He held up the card. Joe took it.

"'Sorry we crushed your dream of singing,'" Joe read aloud.

Nick shook his head, glancing at the card. "While this is freakishly accurate, I don't think a greeting card is going to make everything okay," he said.

Just then Stella walked up to them, an annoyed expression on her face. "Great job, guys," she said. "Macy's devastated."

"Don't worry," Joe told her. "We feel just as terrible as you'd hope."

Nick nodded. "Actually, we feel worse."

"I ate three gallons of chocolate-coma ice cream last night," Kevin added.

Stella sighed. "I have to admit, I feel better that you feel terrible," she said. "But now that I feel better, I feel guilty for feeling good that you feel bad."

"What?" Nick asked, completely confused.

Joe looked smug. "*I* got it," he said proudly.

Stella smiled at him. Then she sighed again. "What I'm trying to say is, I'll talk to Macy for you and try to make everything better."

She started to walk away. But Kevin held out a hand to stop her.

"Wait," he said, squaring his shoulders bravely. "*I'll* talk to Macy. It's what I should have done in the first place."

He looked around, sort of hoping that Macy might be home sick today. Or maybe on vacation in Tahiti. Like, for the rest of the year. That might give him enough time to prepare himself.

But no, there she was. She was shuffling down the hall, dragging a javelin behind her and looking utterly dejected.

"Here I go," he said, trying to sound determined.

"Good luck," Nick told him.

"Thanks. I can do this."

"No, I meant good luck because she's carrying a javelin," Nick clarified.

Kevin decided to ignore that. He walked over

to Macy, who had just stopped and opened her locker.

"Hey, Macy," he greeted her. "Listen, about yesterday. You know how sometimes . . . Um, the thing is . . . It's funny, really, but . . ."

Once again, his attempt to be honest wasn't going well. Kevin decided to start over.

"I want to apologize," he said. "All I was trying to do was not hurt your feelings, and I just made it way worse. I should have been straight with you from the beginning."

For a moment, Macy didn't speak. "I can't believe it," she finally said, sounding touched. "An actual JONAS feels terrible for me?" For a second she looked excited. Then that look faded and she went back to looking devastated. "Aw, I feel bad that you feel terrible!" she exclaimed.

"Okay, okay, okay!" Kevin said quickly. "Let's both stop feeling bad for each other and start again from a good place. Friends?"

"Yay!" Macy cried, instantly going back to looking excited.

In fact, she was so excited that she accidentally slammed her locker door shut with her javelin. Right on Kevin's hand.

He grimaced at the pain. Oh, well. At least it wasn't his foot this time.

"Sorry!" Macy squeaked.

Stella had been watching the whole exchange. Now she walked over, looking puzzled.

"Hey, Macy," she said. "What's going on? I thought you'd still be really upset."

"I feel better because Kevin apologized," Macy explained. Then she frowned slightly as she realized something. "And Stella, none of this would have happened if you hadn't told me I was a good singer in the first place."

Stella gulped. "But you're so sensitive," she protested.

Macy shrugged. "I can handle a little criticism. Remember that basketball game when I missed the shot at the buzzer and we ended up losing by one point?"

Stella shuddered at the memory. "Of course I

PART ONE

Joe and Kevin Lucas put on their best fake smiles—
Stella Malone is approaching, and she does not
look like her usual fashionable self.

Nick tells his brothers and Stella that their favorite
JONAS backup singer is sick!

"Macy, remember the drill. Deep breaths,"
Stella tells Macy Misa, who tends to lose
her cool around JONAS.

Kevin thinks a crisis is the perfect moment
to practice a new song.

Macy practices her singing...without a clue
that she's totally off-key.

Joe tries—and fails—to tell Macy that her singing
isn't exactly up to JONAS standards.

Nick has the perfect card for Macy. It says:
"Sorry we crushed your dream of singing."

Oh, no! Macy accidentally closes a
locker door on Kevin's hand!

PART TWO

Joe, Nick, and Kevin have all ordered pizza from
the same restaurant . . . but why?

Maria, the delivery girl, arrives with the
pizzas. Now Mr. and Mrs. Lucas
understand all the orders!

"That's the Jawbreaker," Joe tells his dad.
"I ordered that one."

"If you guys don't cut back on the pizza, you're
going to have to go out onstage in sweatpants!"
Stella scolds her friends.

The *JONAS Book of Law* clearly states that no member of the band may ask a girl out if another member has a crush on her.

Kevin is ready for his date with Maria. Little does he know that both his brothers have dates with her, too!

"I feel like I bought myself a ticket on the crazy train!" Maria tells the boys when they all confess their crushes.

It's Stella's turn! She swoons as she answers the door—the delivery boy is totally cute!

do," she said. "You were on the front page of every newspaper in the county. We had to eat lunch under the bleachers for two weeks."

"The point is," Macy said, "now I'm the leading scorer in the state. You don't have to treat me like a little helpless bunny."

Stella looked surprised. And also impressed. "You got it," she promised.

Meanwhile, Kevin was still trying to extract his hand from the locker door. Everything he did made it hurt even more.

"And from now on," he said through gritted teeth, "I'm only going to tell the truth. Even if it hurts."

"Really?" Stella said. "So then tell me what you honestly think of my sweater."

She whipped The Sweater out of her bag. That horrible, horrible sweater.

Kevin squirmed, averting his eyes. "I— um, I, uh . . ." he stammered. Then his voice went all high and squeaky. "I *love* it!" he exclaimed.

Stella shook her head. Then she and Macy started to walk away.

"It's so obvious he doesn't like it," Macy commented.

"I know," Stella replied. "His voice gets high when he's lying."

Both girls laughed and glanced over their shoulders at Kevin. His hand was still stuck in the locker door.

"Don't worry about me!" he called after them, his voice higher than ever. Pain also made him go squeaky. "I'm fine! Doesn't hurt a bit!" As soon as the girls were out of earshot, he lowered his voice and glanced at his brothers. "Little help here?"

A couple of days later, Kevin slunk through the school hallways trying not to meet anyone's eye. That had nothing to do with his hand, which had almost returned to its normal size and color by now. It had *everything* to do with the sweater he was wearing. It looked exactly like Stella's sweater. Her horrible, horrible sweater.

Macy was heading toward the atrium carrying a small radio when she spotted him. She took a deep breath to calm herself down. Even after all that had happened, she still practically fainted every time she spotted a JONAS. Let alone tried to talk to one.

"Hey, Kevin," she said. "Nice sweater."

Kevin sighed, sounding defeated. "Stella made it especially for me because I said I liked hers so much." He shot a dull look at Macy's radio. "Where are you headed?"

"I was thinking," Macy replied, "I love singing so much, I don't see why I have to stop just because I'm terrible at it."

Kevin brightened a little. He was glad to see that Macy hadn't been scarred for life by what had happened. Unlike his hand. And his eardrums. And his retinas . . . He glanced down at his own sweater before quickly looking away again.

"That's a great attitude," he told Macy. "Share your passion with the world!"

Macy smiled. "Well, maybe not with the *whole* world."

Before Kevin could ask what she meant, she hurried ahead into the atrium. She closed the door behind her and hung a sign on it reading DANGER—DO NOT ENTER.

Then she hit PLAY on the radio. Kevin watched as she opened her mouth.

Fortunately, the glass kept him from hearing a note. But he could tell that she was singing. Leaves started falling from the trees, flowers wilted all around her, and several passing birds thudded to the ground.

And all the while, Kevin just smiled, happy to see his friend happy.

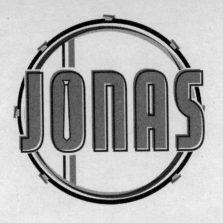

PART
TWO

CHAPTER ONE

It was almost dinnertime at the converted firehouse the Lucas family called home. Tom Lucas and his wife, Sandy, were in the kitchen. So was their youngest son, Frankie.

"Hey, hon," Mr. Lucas said hungrily, "how about you whip up a batch of your famous spaghetti with Sandy sauce for dinner?"

Mrs. Lucas shot him a look. "By 'whip up a batch,' you mean stand over a boiling pot for six hours sweating my freckles off?"

Mr. Lucas grinned sheepishly. "Honey, you obviously misheard me. What I meant was, we should have burgers. That I make. Right now."

He hurried over to the refrigerator and swung open the door. Bending over, he started rooting around inside, looking for burger ingredients.

Frankie watched with interest. He loved burgers. He also loved his mother's freckles. If having burgers meant she got to keep them instead of sweating them off, he was all for it. He licked his lips. His stomach growled. Then it rang.

Oops, that wasn't his stomach. It was the doorbell.

Mrs. Lucas turned to answer it. Well, she *thought* about *starting* to turn to answer it. Before she could actually move a muscle, her son Joe came dropping down one of the three fire poles that connected the main floor with the loft above.

"That's for me!" Joe announced. "I ordered pizza."

A second later Joe's younger brother, Nick,

dropped down the second pole. "That's for me!" he exclaimed. "I ordered pizza."

The oldest Lucas brother, Kevin, came skidding down the third pole. "That's for me!" he shouted. "I ordered pizza."

Safely on the ground, all three of them paused and eyed one another suspiciously. Meanwhile Mrs. Lucas followed through on her earlier plan and headed toward the door.

"Here's a thought," she said to Frankie and Mr. Lucas over her shoulder. "How about pizza?" Then she glanced at her three older sons. "Where'd you guys order from?"

"Picarillo's," all three answered in unison.

They paused again. And eyed one another even *more* suspiciously.

"Not PUKE-ARILLOS!" Frankie cried. He began pretending to throw up.

Mrs. Lucas looked pretty disgusted, too, and, surprisingly, it had nothing to do with Frankie's fake puking. "That place?" she said. "Their pizza's terrible!"

"Terrible?" Kevin exclaimed, sounding wounded.

"How can you say that?" Nick's lower lip quivered slightly with dismay.

Mrs. Lucas was worried. Kevin, Joe, and Nick made up the superpopular band JONAS. Their faces—which were undeniably cute—could be found on a dozen magazine covers at any given time, and their voices were always on the radio. But so far, even their fabulous success hadn't changed them much. They still lived at home between tours, attended an ordinary high school, and helped out with the chores—most of the time. Totally normal.

But this? Definitely *not* normal. Had success finally gone to their heads? Turned them into weird celebrities who actually *liked* bad pizza?

As she pondered that terrible possibility, Mrs. Lucas opened the door. A delivery boy was standing there holding three pizza boxes.

As Mrs. Lucas reached for some money, the pizza-delivery boy took off his hat. Waves of silky brown hair came cascading down around his shoulders. Er, *her* shoulders. Mrs. Lucas realized the pizza-delivery boy was actually a pizza-delivery *girl*.

And her sons realized it, too. Most definitely.

"It's the most beautiful pizza in the world!" Joe said with a dreamy sigh, gazing adoringly at the pizza-delivery girl.

Nick and Kevin were gazing dreamily, too.

"*Now* I understand why we ordered from Picarillo's," Mrs. Lucas said. Yes, she understood *perfectly*.

CHAPTER TWO

A short while later, the entire family, except for Nick—who claimed he had a headache and needed to rest—was at the dinner table eating. Or trying to, at least. The pizza wasn't making it easy.

"Well, it *is* round," Mrs. Lucas said dubiously. "And there's something melted on it. Yet I can't bring myself to call it pizza."

Mr. Lucas looked disheartened. "I keep

chewing and chewing, but I just can't get it down."

"That's the 'jawbreaker,'" Joe said proudly. "I ordered that one."

He reached over and switched plates with his father. For a second, Mr. Lucas just looked relieved to have an empty plate in front of him. But he was still hungry. Reaching for a slice from one of the non-jawbreaker boxes, he stared at it suspiciously. It bubbled back at him, looking menacing. Also gross.

"I can't believe this stuff!" Mr. Lucas cried. It must break some cooking or taste code, he mused silently.

Joe shrugged. "Hey, where is it written that pizza always has to taste . . . good?" he asked philosophically.

"Yeah," Kevin put in. "And Picarillo's is environmentally friendly. Their slogan is, 'We use the stuff other places throw out.'"

Mr. Lucas rolled his eyes and set down the slice. This was ridiculous. "Would your sudden love of Picarillo's have anything to do with the cute delivery girl?"

"Who?" Kevin asked innocently.

"Oh, was the delivery girl a girl?" Joe added even more innocently.

Mrs. Lucas noticed that Frankie wasn't eating. "Have some pizza, honey," she urged him.

Frankie glared at her. "Why do you hate me?" That was the only reason he could see for this joke of a meal.

Just then the doorbell rang again. Mr. Lucas got up after wrestling free of some stretchy cheese that was trying to glue his hands to the table.

"I'll get it," he said. "Anything to escape from this cheese prison."

He headed over to the door. When he opened it, a delivery man was standing there. Mr. Lucas looked a little closer. Yep, definitely a man. And he smelled like food. Chinese food, to be exact.

By then Frankie was rushing for the door. He was smiling.

"Frankie loves the mu shu!" he crowed as he paid the delivery man. Then he grabbed the bags the man was carrying and took off in the direction of his room.

"Hey, Franks!" Mrs. Lucas called after him. "Where are you going with that? How much did you order? Let Mom get you a plate . . . or two . . ."

She grabbed a couple of empty plates and took off after Frankie.

As he watched them go, Mr. Lucas felt like kicking himself. Why hadn't he grabbed that Chinese food when he had the chance? Sure, Frankie was quick and absurdly clever. But Mr. Lucas was taller and stronger. He could have had most of that mu shu down the hatch before the kid could figure out what to do. And he wouldn't even feel bad about it. In an emergency situation like this, it was every Lucas for himself. . . .

But it was too late now. With a sigh, Mr. Lucas swung the door shut.

RRRRING!

The doorbell rang again. Mr. Lucas felt a flare

of hope. Had the Chinese food delivery man returned with more mu shu? This time, he'd be ready. . . .

He swung open the door. But it wasn't the delivery man. It was the Picarillo's delivery girl!

"*Gaaaah!*" Mr. Lucas exclaimed, his dreams of actual food fizzling out. "What are you doing back here?"

"Delivering pizzas," the girl replied. "It's kind of my job. I deliver pizzas. And solve crime." She shrugged. "But mostly the pizza thing."

Suddenly Nick came thudding down one of the fire poles. "I just texted Picarillo's," he announced.

"Me, too!" Joe added in surprise.

Kevin didn't say anything for a moment. He was bent over his cell phone. "And . . . send," he muttered, hitting a button.

Nick frowned at him. "Dude, she's already here!"

Mr. Lucas just sighed. Then he paid for the pizzas.

Meanwhile Joe had sidled closer. He had his

best Mr. Smooth smile on his face and was wearing some of his sharpest casual clothes. "What's new, Maria?" he asked the delivery girl.

"Since you saw me twelve minutes ago?" Maria asked. "Let's see: I raced back to the shop, grabbed the pizza, bragged that I was delivering to JONAS, got a flat tire, fixed it, and beat my best time by thirty seconds."

Joe looked impressed. "Wow. And all I've done is eat!" He gazed at her soulfully. "I like your pizza-delivery hat, Maria."

Nick pushed forward to join him. He was gazing at Maria even more soulfully. That wasn't surprising. After all, it was well known that he was the most soulful member of JONAS.

"I like your pizza-delivery hat *and* your Picarillo's T-shirt, Maria," he added.

Not to be outdone by his younger brothers, Kevin hurried over. "Maria, I like your inner beauty," he said earnestly. "And your zit-free complexion."

Maria giggled. "You guys are so funny!" she

exclaimed. "I wish I could hang, but I should get to my next delivery. There's nothing worse than cold pizza."

She waved and exited. Standing in the doorway, the three brothers stared off after her.

Mr. Lucas glanced from the mess awaiting him back at the table to the boxes of new, hot, steaming mess in his hands. Then he pushed past to join his sons in the doorway. There was something that had to be said. . . .

"I think temperature is the *least* of your problems!" he shouted after Maria.

CHAPTER THREE

Joe groaned. He'd never been so full in his life. Beside him, Kevin groaned, too. The two of them were lying immobile. They'd been eating Picarillo's pizza almost nonstop since the night before.

The sound of approaching footsteps stopped their groans momentarily. However, it was too much effort for either brother to turn and see who it was.

"If I have to keep making your pants bigger, the world is going to have a denim shortage!" the voice that went with the footsteps said, sounding irritated.

Joe let out another groan. He knew that voice. It was Stella Malone. She was the brothers' life-long friend as well as the stylist for their band. She took clothes seriously. *Very* seriously. Usually the guys appreciated that. It kept them looking like rock stars at all times.

Right now, though, Joe and Kevin wished that Stella took their clothes a little *less* seriously. Or at least a little more quietly. Her yelling made their heads hurt, which made their stomachs hurt even more than they already did.

"Our pants fit fine," Joe mumbled, still lying there motionless.

Kevin was motionless, too. "As long as we don't move," he said.

R-R-R-R-RIP!

"Or breathe," Kevin added.

Stella rolled her eyes. "If you guys don't cut

back on the pizza, you're going to have to go out onstage in sweatpants."

"Oooh!" Kevin said, intrigued. "Power sliding in sweatpants. Awesome!"

"You could design us some really cool ones," Joe suggested. "With special pockets to hold our pizza."

All Stella could do was shake her head. She didn't have time for this conversation. It looked like she had pants to let out—again.

As she hurried off, Mr. Lucas entered. He was shuffling through a handful of receipts.

"Gentlemen, a word," he said, his expression stern.

Just then Nick came in. He was tying the waistband of the sweatpants he was wearing.

"Hey, have you guys tried sweatpants?" he asked his brothers, unaware that his father did *not* look happy. "There's a lot more room!"

Mr. Lucas frowned at him. "Okay," he said, turning to frown at his other sons. "Apparently, in the past month we've spent over five hundred dollars on Picarillo's quote-unquote pizza."

The guys mumbled their disbelief: "What?"

"We didn't spend that much!"

"No way!"

Before Mr. Lucas could confirm, there was a rustle of cardboard from a corner of the room. Glancing over, he saw Frankie sticking his head out of a large, elaborate homemade fort. It was built entirely of Picarillo's pizza boxes.

"Hey!" Frankie protested. "I'm trying to sleep!"

He ducked back inside his fort. Mr. Lucas sighed and returned his attention to his older sons.

"Look," he said as patiently as he could, "I get that you all have a crush on the delivery girl, but—"

"Crush?" Joe interrupted incredulously. "On the delivery girl?"

He laughed. It sounded a little forced. Nick and Kevin laughed, too. It sounded *really* forced.

Mr. Lucas started wandering around the room. There was pizza everywhere. Under the table.

Inside one of Kevin's guitars. Even rotating in the slot of the CD player. Mr. Lucas gathered up as much of it as he could. The trash bin was too good for this stuff. Maybe he could build a pizza bonfire and burn it.

"This is no fake-laughing matter," he warned the guys. "The pizza party is over. Nobody's ordering any more of it." Shooting his sons one last stern look, he left the loft.

Their dad had sounded pretty serious. Sighing, Kevin, Joe, and Nick started picking up more cold pizza slices. They tossed them in a pile on the table. There *were* quite a few slices. . . .

"Imagine Dad thinking I have a crush on the pizza girl," Joe exclaimed. He paused, his eyes taking on a faraway look. "Just because Maria has hair as shiny as eggplant . . ."

"And she smells delicious," Nick put in. "Like toasted oregano."

Kevin nodded. "And she smells delicious. Like toasted—" He stopped himself, shooting a look at Nick. "Oh. That's what you just said."

They all picked up a few more slices. Then Joe let out a loud sigh.

"I miss her so much!" he exclaimed. "If I can't order from Picarillo's, how will I see the pizza girl again?" Then his expression brightened. "Duh! I'll just call Maria and ask her out!" He reached for his cell phone.

"Not if I call her first!" Nick blurted out, grabbing his own phone out of his pocket.

"I've got you both beat!" Kevin bragged. His phone was already in his hand. Before the others could react, he pressed one of the speed dial buttons.

Joe's phone rang. He answered it. "Hello?"

Kevin spoke into his own phone. "Hey, Joe," he said. "Do you have the number to Picarillo's?"

Nick had had enough. "Okay, everybody, hang up!" he ordered.

Even though he was the youngest of the three, the others almost always obeyed Nick when he used that tone of voice. They both hung up.

"Nobody's asking Maria out," Nick continued with a frown. "May I remind you of the *JONAS Book of Law*? Kevin?"

He glanced toward his oldest brother. Kevin nodded and headed over to a bookshelf. Peering at the books, he reached up and selected one. It was leather-bound, ancient, and dusty. *Very* dusty.

Kevin tried to blow off the dust and ending up blowing it right up into his own face. He coughed. "Too much fake dust!" he complained.

Nick just tapped his foot, waiting. "Amendment three," he reminded Kevin. "Subparagraph A. Line six."

Kevin opened the book. Pulling out a magnifying glass, he started to read aloud.

"'It was a dark and stormy night,'" he intoned. "'Fireball the pony was lost in Box Canyon—'"

He cut himself off. That didn't sound right. Shutting the book, he checked the spine.

"Oops. Wrong book," he announced.

He grabbed another dusty old book off the shelf. This time he checked the cover before opening it. It was titled *JONAS Book of Law*.

With a satisfied nod, Kevin flipped it to the appropriate page. Once again, he started to read aloud:

"'If more than one JONAS is crushing on the same girl, absolutely *no* JONAS may ask out said crushee, or JONAS risks destroying the bond that makes them awesome bandmates and brothers.'"

As the law sank in, Nick nodded. "Yeah, we don't want to destroy our awesomeness."

Joe still looked a little dreamy. "But what if the crushee is the beautiful and adorable Maria?"

"Well, then we have a problem," Nick said.

Kevin shrugged hopelessly. "How do you solve a problem like Maria?"

"There's no problem," Joe said firmly, snapping out of his dreaminess. "The JONAS law is clear. None of us are going out with Maria. Agreed?"

He stuck out one hand. Nick put his on top of it.

"No more bad pizza," Nick agreed.

Kevin placed his hand on top of Nick's. "No more tight pants."

Then, together, the three of them threw up their hands. "Noooooooo Maria!" they all cried in one voice.

CHAPTER FOUR

THUMP!

Nick landed softly at the bottom of the fire pole. The kitchen was dark and deserted. Excellent.

He caught his reflection in a mirror on the wall. Pausing, he admired his outfit. He straightened his tie and ran his fingers through his curly hair until it was perfect. Excellent.

ZZZZZZIP!

The soft sound made him turn. One of the kitchen chairs had just spun around, revealing Joe. He was sitting there, his fingertips pressed together like a villain in some cheesy spy movie.

"Well, well, well," Joe said, sounding just as villainy as he looked. "Good evening, Mr. Nick."

Nick froze, his heart pounding.

"If I didn't know any better," Joe continued, "I'd say somebody's dressed for a date. Perhaps with a girl I like to call . . . *Maria*?"

Nick squared his shoulders. He wasn't going down without a fight. Not when the stakes were this high. This could be true love. He felt it in his bones. Maria was cool. And funny. And didn't go all weird because they were in a famous band. *And* she could probably get them free pizza anytime they wanted. Yup, she was worth fighting for. He had to play this perfectly.

"Can't a guy get dressed up for his evening snack?" he said, doing his best to sound casual. He headed for the refrigerator, trying to throw Joe off his trail.

"Oh, please," Joe mocked. "I can smell your body spray from here." He paused and sniffed. "What is that, 'Le Babe Magnet'?"

"For your information, it's called Growl," Nick corrected him. Then he squinted, taking a better look at Joe. Wait a second. What was that sticking out of his shirt pocket? "And it looks to me like *you're* the one going on a date with Maria!"

Leaping forward, he grabbed at Joe's pocket. Aha! Just as he'd thought!

"Pizza coupons!" Nick spat out accusingly, waving the coupons in the air. "Care to explain these?"

"Certainly," Joe said calmly. "You present these when you pay, and you get a discount on your pizza."

THUMP!

Nick and Joe turned. Kevin had just dropped down one of the poles. He was stylishly dressed and carrying flowers. As soon as he saw his brothers staring at him, he stuck the flowers behind his back.

"What's up, bros?" he asked.

Joe glared at him. "What's behind your back?"

"Uh . . . flowers?" Kevin said, pulling them back out. He searched his mind desperately for a cover story. "I'm trying to attract bees."

"But you're allergic to bees," Joe reminded him.

Kevin searched his mind again. Nope. He had nothing. Bees it was.

"True," he said. "But unless you want to give me time to come up with another excuse, that's what I'm going with."

"Looks like we're all sneak-dating Maria," Nick spoke up. "So much for Amendment Three, subparagraph A, line six."

"We've never *not* obeyed the JONAS law," Joe pointed out. "We're lawless. We're like outlaws."

They all stared at one another for a moment, trying on the idea of being outlaws. It felt not entirely comfortable.

Kevin was the first to break the silence. "I think we should all ask her out," he said.

Nick nodded. "And may the best man impress her, uh, the best."

"Totally," Joe agreed.

So it was decided. JONAS was breaking their own law, regardless of the consequences.

Nick figured there was no point in wasting time. He reached for his cell phone.

"Oh, no!" Joe said when he noticed. "*I'm* calling her first!"

He pulled out his own cell phone. But Kevin was grinning triumphantly, his phone already in his hand.

"I've got you both beat!" he crowed.

He hit speed dial. A second later Joe's phone rang.

"Hello?" Joe said into it.

Kevin pressed his own phone to his face. "Hey," he said. "I lost that number to Picarillo's. Can you help me out?"

CHAPTER FIVE

The next day at school, Kevin spotted Stella and her best friend, Macy Misa, walking down the hallway. Macy was a star athlete. At the moment, she was carrying an oar. Kevin guessed it had something to do with the crew team. But he wasn't really focused on that. He had more important things on his mind.

"Stella!" he called, hurrying over to them. "You're a girl."

"Last time I checked," Stella agreed.

"How do I impress one?" Kevin asked, ignoring her sarcastic tone.

Macy gazed at him adoringly. "Just existing pretty much does it," she answered for Stella.

Sometimes, Stella had to admit, she found Macy's JONAS obsession a little tiresome. But this time the girl had a point. "Why do *you* need advice on impressing a girl?" she asked Kevin.

"I'm going up against two real 'playahs'," Kevin explained. "I need every advantage I can get."

That sounded a little odd to Stella. What kind of guy could go up against a JONAS? It didn't matter. She loved giving advice—fashion or otherwise.

"Well," she said, "I find it's always impressive when a boy cooks for me."

Kevin nodded eagerly. This was exactly what he was looking for! He pulled out a pad and paper and started taking notes.

"Excellent," he said. "What do they usually cook?"

"Well, it's never actually happened," Stella admitted. "But I think if it did, I'd be impressed."

Kevin jotted another note. "Does cereal count?" he asked.

Stella had to stop and think about that. "The thought counts," she decided at last.

"I'd eat the cereal!" Macy put in eagerly. In her excitement, she banged her oar on the floor. Well, not the *floor* so much as what happened to be *between* the oar and the floor. Which happened to be Kevin's foot.

Kevin yelped in pain. He yanked his foot to safety. He always seemed to get hurt when he was around Macy.

"Sorry," Macy said. She shrugged. "But I'd still eat the cereal."

Later that day, Stella and Macy were waiting by the school elevator. Crew practice was over, and now Macy was carrying a lacrosse stick.

"Stella!" someone called.

Turning, Stella saw Nick racing over. Reflexively, he ducked as he reached them. He was just in time. Macy had turned around, too, and her lacrosse stick whooshed right over his head. It made his curls quiver.

"I need some advice," Nick said breathlessly, straightening again. "I'm trying to get close to a girl."

Macy had been waiting to hear those words all her life. She was a girl! She stepped closer, pressing herself up to Nick.

Nick glanced at her. "A *specific* girl," he clarified quickly.

"Oh." Macy stepped back.

Nick returned his attention to Stella. "The problem is, there are these two 'mack daddies' who are also interested in her," he explained.

"Wait a minute." Stella held up one hand. Things were suddenly starting to become clearer. She peered at Nick. "My Stella senses are tingling. Would these two 'mack daddies' be Kevin and Joe?"

Nick looked impressed. "Mack dangit, you're good!"

Stella's expression was grim. "Emergency JONAS meeting," she ordered. "In three . . . two . . . one," Stella finished a few minutes later.

Inside the hallway, Kevin, Nick, and Joe were lined up. Macy was looking on from nearby. By now, she was carrying an archery set.

Stella surveyed the three members of JONAS. First Kevin. Then Nick. Finally her gaze stopped on Joe. Her eyes narrowed.

"What is this I'm hearing about some girl you're going to ask out?" she demanded.

Joe held up a finger in a "one second" gesture. Then he stepped over and carefully removed Macy's bow and arrow from her hands. Better safe than sorry.

After setting the archery set aside, he returned to his spot in front of Stella. She looked annoyed. *Really* annoyed. Even more annoyed than she'd been when Kevin had ripped the knees out of a brand-new pair of custom-made pants while practicing his power slide. Could this be her roundabout way of starting another pants rant?

Joe glanced at his brothers' pants. Then he checked his own. Nope. All six knees were totally intact. So that wasn't it. It *was* the girl-he-was-going-to-ask-out thing. Interesting.

"Who told you that?" he asked.

Stella waved a hand toward Nick and Kevin. "Mack and Daddy," she replied. She frowned at Joe. "Who is this girl?"

Uh-oh. Nick and Kevin exchanged a glance. Everyone knew that Stella and Joe liked each other. Well, everyone, that is, except maybe Stella and Joe.

"You don't know her," Joe told Stella with a shrug. He couldn't understand why Stella only seemed mad at *him*.

"Is she pretty?" Stella demanded.

Joe rolled his eyes. "No, she's hideous. Why else would I ask her out?"

"Come on," Stella urged. "Tell me who she is!"

Joe smirked. "Why?" he asked playfully. "Are you jealous?"

"Of course not!" Stella snapped. She paused. "Is it that new girl in home ec?"

"Is it Macy on the archery squad?" Macy asked, doing her best to throw her voice as if Stella had asked the question.

Nick was feeling impatient. Maria was somewhere out there. All alone. Probably lonely. Just waiting to be asked out . . .

"Are Kevin and Nick still in trouble, or can we go?" he asked, taking a step forward.

Stella glared at him. He stepped back into line. Guess they were staying.

"Let me fill you guys in on some female 4-1-1," Stella said. "If one guy likes a girl, that's cool. If two guys like a girl, even better. If three guys like a girl, jackpot. But if all three guys happen to be brothers . . ." She paused for effect. "Well, she just bought herself a ticket on the crazy train."

"But what do we do?" Kevin protested. "All three of us like her."

Stella crossed her arms over her chest. "Well, all three of you had better *un*like her."

"We talked about it," Nick said, trying to sound confident. "And we can handle it."

"You can handle going after the same girl?" Stella shook her head in disbelief. She knew better. "Remember when all three of you fought over that teddy bear you used to have when you were little?"

Nick blinked. Joe tilted his head to one side. Kevin gazed thoughtfully at a locker. All three of them were drifting back to that memory. Drifting . . . drifting . . .

"I got it first!" Joe squealed, yanking on one limb of a teddy bear.

"I'm the oldest!" Kevin yanked on another limb.

Nick was clinging to yet another limb. "Mr. Bumble belongs to me!" he howled.

The teddy bear looked dismayed. Its arms and legs were stretching . . . stre-e-e-e-etching . . .

Nick snapped back to the here and now. "That's one of the few times we really got mad at each other," he remembered.

Stella nodded. "It tore you apart for a month," she reminded all three of them. "And this isn't a teddy bear. It's a girl. A real girl. With real arms."

Kevin shuddered, picturing Maria's arms stretching like Mr. Bumble's had. "She's right," he told Nick and Kevin. "Let's not go there again."

"I'm glad you've come to your senses." Stella smiled, looking satisfied. She knew the boys would listen to her. They usually did. "Come on, Macy."

As soon as the girls had disappeared, Nick turned to his brothers. "Okay," he said briskly. "We can't all go out with Maria at the same time. We'll end up fighting."

Kevin nodded sadly. "I wish she could just come over, hang out, and decide who she likes best."

"You're such a dreamer, Kev," Joe said with a laugh, shaking his head.

But Nick brightened. He'd just had one of his patented brilliant ideas.

"How about if we ask her to come over, hang out, and decide·whom she likes best?" he suggested.

Joe gasped. "Nick, you're a genius!"

Kevin frowned. "Hey!" Hadn't he just said that?

CHAPTER SIX

Later that day, the guys were hanging out in the kitchen at home. Nick checked his watch.

"Maria should be here any minute," he said. "Best behavior—right, bros?"

Joe looked worried. "What if one of us starts to flirt?"

Nick saw his point. It would be hard to resist that urge when Maria was around. Especially for his brothers. Joe definitely had a weak spot when it came to the ladies. And Kevin? Well, you just never knew how Kevin was going to react. Usually that was part of his charm. But right now, with Maria on her way, it worried Nick.

"Maybe we should have a code phrase," he said. "Like . . . 'the phone's ringing.'"

Kevin stood up. "I'll get it."

"No," Nick told him. "That's the code phrase. If one of us says 'the phone's ringing,' that means you're hitting on Maria too hard."

The doorbell rang. Joe jumped to his feet.

"I'll bet that's Maria," he said. "I'll get it."

Kevin was already hurrying for the door. "I'll get it."

"Let's all three get it." Nick rushed after them.

When they opened the door, Maria was standing outside. She was holding a pizza.

"Maria, so glad you could come over and hang with us," Joe said in his smoothest voice.

Maria smiled. "It felt weird coming over here without a pizza in my hand," she said. "So I brought some pizza."

Suddenly Frankie appeared. "All right!" he exclaimed. "A new deck for my condo!"

He grabbed the pizza box and took off. The others watched him go. Then they all went inside and sat down.

There was a moment of silence. All the three Lucas guys could do was stare at Maria. She was awesome. And adorable. And totally, fantastically gorgeous . . .

"You know, Maria," Joe said, still sounding suave, "if I could rearrange the alphabet, I'd put *U* and *I* together."

Kevin and Nick traded a glance. "The phone's ringing," Nick said.

Maria looked confused. "I don't hear a phone."

Joe was still gazing at her adoringly. "Me, neither." The code was lost on him.

Kevin jumped to his feet. "Be right back!" he said, heading toward the kitchen.

Joe's gaze never left Maria. If he had his way, it would never leave her for the rest of their lives. She was just that perfect.

"Do you like motorcycles, Maria?" he asked. "Because you'd look good in my sidecar."

"Oh," Maria said. "That sounds cool."

Nick's teeth were clenched so hard he was afraid his jaw might crack. "The phone is ringing," he told Joe—again.

"There's no phone ringing," Maria told him. "You've done too many rock concerts."

Just then Kevin returned. He was carrying a tray with a bowl on it. "Hungry, Maria?" he asked, setting it down. "I cooked for you. Hope you like Crunchy Caps!"

Nick was surprised as he stared at the bowl of cereal. He'd assumed Kevin had just gone to answer the nonringing phone.

A moment later, a sound came out of Kevin's pocket. It was a tinny little voice accompanied by music. The voice kept repeating "Kevin likes Maria . . . Kevin likes Maria . . ."

Kevin was still smiling dopily at Maria. "It's my new ringtone," he explained.

He grabbed the phone out of his pocket

and checked the caller ID. Then he turned and glared at Nick. Nick was holding his own cell phone.

Maria looked more confused than ever. "Did you just call him?" she asked Nick.

"Uh, yes," Nick told her. "I wanted to tell him that . . ." He fished around for a cover story. Then another brilliant idea came to him. One of his patented two-birds-with-one-stone strokes of genius. "I just wrote you a song!"

That snapped Joe out of his Maria coma. He stopped gazing at her and started glaring at Nick. He knew what would happen if Nick actually *had* written a song. He'd sing it. Marie would swoon. And Joe would have no chance.

"The phone is ringing!" he snapped. "The phone is ringing! The phone is absolutely, way, *way* ringing!"

But Nick was already pulling a guitar out from behind the couch. This was perfect! Why hadn't he thought of it earlier? Singing Maria a song would really showcase his intense, sensitive side. How could she possibly resist that?

"It's nothing, really," he told her modestly. "Just a little something I came up with."

He strummed a chord. Then another. He closed his eyes and started to sing. It felt as if he and Maria were alone. . . .

"Not cool, Nick," Joe snapped.

"Well, I wouldn't have had to sing to her if you hadn't been all 'Hey, Maria, I have a motorcycle,'" Nick argued, forgetting that Maria was still right there.

Joe flapped a hand in Kevin's direction. "Well, *I* wouldn't have had to bring up the motorcycle if Captain Suave over here hadn't broken out the cereal."

"You started it!" Kevin protested. "'*U* and *I* together.'" He shook his head in annoyance. "Like you could really rearrange the alphabet!"

"Uh . . ." Maria broke in, "all this attention is kind of flattering, but mostly weird. So I think I should go home." She stood up.

"Wait, Maria," Kevin said. Then he glanced at

his brothers, looking troubled. "She's right," he told them. "It's Mr. Bumble all over again. She's a stretched-out teddy bear!"

Maria looked alarmed. That didn't sound good. "Look," she said, backing away. "I don't know who Mr. Bumble is, and I don't want to know."

She turned and hurried toward the door. The guys jumped up and followed.

"Wait, Maria," Joe called. "We're sorry about tonight, but we've never broken the sacred book of JONAS law."

"The sacred what of JONAS who?" Maria asked. She shook her head, looking overwhelmed. "Fake phones, Mr. Bumble, JONAS law. I feel like I bought myself a ticket on the crazy train!"

She turned and kept going toward the door. "Maria!" Nick called after her. "We can explain! It's just that all three of us like you."

"Maybe we can share you," Kevin suggested.

Maria looked more alarmed than ever. "I'm

out of here," she said. Then, without another word, she disappeared out the door.

Nick sighed and turned to his brothers. "Maybe explaining wasn't the way to go."

CHAPTER SEVEN

Later, the guys were up in their room helping Stella organize their clothes. But their minds weren't really on the task at hand.

Nick picked up a shirt. He started to fold it the normal way. Halfway through, he forgot what he was doing and ended up rolling it into a ball.

Nearby, Kevin was supposed to be sorting through some shoes. Instead he was just staring into space.

Joe tried to hang up a pair of pants on a rack. But he wasn't paying enough attention. The pants slid off the hanger and onto the floor.

"Joe, careful!" Stella cried. "The crease in those pants is razor sharp, and you're not wearing safety gloves."

Joe apologized insincerely. He couldn't seem to care about anyone except . . .

Nick sighed. "I can't believe we were ready to turn our backs on the sacred book of JONAS law for a girl."

"Even if it *was* Maria with hair like silky strands of mozzarella," Joe said dreamily.

"She was a big part of our lives," Kevin added wistfully.

Stella rolled her eyes. She set aside the clothes she was holding. Enough was enough. This behavior was just downright foolish.

"Okay, pop quiz," she said. "What color are Maria's eyes?"

"Blue?" Joe guessed.

"Brown?" Nick tried.

Kevin shrugged. "I'm pretty sure she had two."

"Name one thing she did other than deliver pizza," Stella said, challenging them with yet another "tough" question.

"Um . . ." Joe thought about that. "She rang the doorbell?"

Nick smiled. "She smelled good."

"She delivered garlic bread," Kevin said.

"Hello?" Stella put her hands on her hips and stared at them. "Don't you guys get it?"

Kevin was starting to get the same feeling he always got during pop quizzes in math class. Namely, the panicky feeling of not knowing the right answers.

"How can we get it if you keep asking us questions?" he cried.

Stella sighed. As usual, she was going to have to spell it out for them. "You were fighting over a girl you hardly knew," she said, speaking slowly and clearly so they'd be sure to follow her. "It wasn't about Maria at all."

Joe looked pensive. Maybe Stella was right.

After all, she usually was. "I guess we did get a little overly competitive," he admitted.

"And you guys aren't about being competitive," Stella said. "You're about teamwork. That's what makes you a great band."

Kevin smiled. Suddenly he didn't feel like he was in math class anymore. "Okay, now we get it," he said.

"I got it a while ago," Nick informed him smugly.

"Me, too," Joe put in quickly. "I was just waiting for you guys to catch up."

Nick glanced at Stella. "We promise not to be so competitive," he assured her.

Kevin nodded vigorously. "And I'm going to be even less competitive than these guys."

"Dude," Joe said, "there's no way you're going to be less competitive than me!"

"First one down the fire poles is the least competitive!" Nick cried.

The three of them leaped for the poles and disappeared. A second later, their voices floated upward. "I won!" all three cried at the same time.

Stella smacked her own forehead in disbelief. Why did she even bother? Boys were always going to be boys—even if they were famous.

CHAPTER EIGHT

Later that day, Nick put his left hand on the *JONAS Book of Law*. Beside him, Joe stepped forward and did the same. Then Kevin added his hand to the dusty old book.

All three of them were in the firehouse kitchen. Stella was watching from nearby.

"We solemnly swear to never, ever let a girl come between us again," Nick intoned. "No matter how cute, funny, or how little we know about her."

"Word," Joe and Kevin agreed.

Stella smiled. "I'm proud of you guys."

"Me, too," Joe said.

Just then, the doorbell rang. Joe headed over to answer it.

"*I'm* more proud of us," Nick said.

Joe glanced over his shoulder. "My middle *name* is 'Proud.'"

"My middle name is 'More-Proud-Than-Nick-And-Joe,'" Kevin put in quickly. "It's a long name—that's why I don't use it very often."

Stella hardly heard them. She was still mulling over the whole ridiculous Maria situation.

"When you think about it," she mused, "it's pretty silly how hard you fell over someone you didn't even know."

By then Joe was swinging open the door. Standing outside was a uniformed delivery person.

"Who ordered from the Juice King?" Joe called over his shoulder.

Kevin shook his head. He hadn't ordered any

juice. Nick shrugged. He didn't even like the Juice King. They used too much banana.

Just then the delivery person took off his cap. His hair came tumbling out in a gleaming cascade of hotness. Yes, *his* hair. The delivery person was a totally adorable *guy*.

Stella smiled, her eyes going all gooey. "I did," she swooned.

Hey, she never said she was perfect.

Don't miss a beat! Check out the next book in the JONAS series.

⸱DOUBLE TAKE

Adapted by Marianne Schaberg

Based on the series created by Michael Curtis & Roger S. H. Schulman

Part One is based on the episode, "That Ding You Do!" Written by Heather MacGillvray & Linda Mathious

It was just a typical afternoon in the Lucas household. Kevin, Nick, and Joe were lounging in their living room together.

The boys lived in a converted firehouse with their parents and younger brother, Frankie. Having to slide down a pole to reach the breakfast table wasn't the only thing that set the three Lucas brothers apart from other teenagers—they also happened to be mega rock stars. They were so famous that their pictures were plastered on the walls of the rooms of teenage girls' everywhere. Together, the three brothers made up the hottest rock band on the planet, JONAS.

That afternoon, Kevin, the oldest member of JONAS, was working on his pecs, lifting twenty-pound weights in the corner. He needed to stay fit if he was going to jam out practically every night onstage. Nick sat on a stool strumming his guitar, practicing a new song for the band. Sprawled out on the couch, Joe wasn't working quite so hard; he was busy catching up on the latest issue of *Teenster Magazine*.

"Hey, guys, there's a new 'How well do you know JONAS?' quiz in here!" Joe called out, flipping to a page in the magazine. He always got a kick out of the questions and answers. "Let's see how well I know . . . Joe!"

Joe went through each question aloud: "Yes . . . No . . . Armadillo . . . No . . . Yes."

Clutching the magazine, Joe jumped up on the couch. "All right! Five out of five! I'm a"—he searched for his score—"'real Joe nut,'" he read.

Curious, Kevin and Nick walked over to check out the quiz. Reading over Joe's shoulder, Nick raised an eyebrow. "Hey, your favorite snack isn't cherry pudding," he said to Kevin.

Kevin shook his head. "It's chocolate tacos. And your favorite color isn't medium spring green. It's electric indigo," he told Nick as he flopped down on the couch, dejected.

Pulling the magazine away again, Kevin read his profile. Everything was wrong! This meant war! "We need to straighten out *Teenster Magazine!*" he cried.

Excited by the prospect of putting the magazine in its place, Kevin turned to his brothers and went on. "We should write a letter to the editor," he said and searched for the name in the magazine.

Joe was as eager as his brothers to prove a point to the magazine—even if it had gotten some of *his* favorites right. "Who's got a pen?" he asked.

Fumbling through his pockets, Nick shook his head. No luck. Kevin shrugged. He didn't have a pen either. Within seconds, Joe had a solution; he jumped up and ran over to one of the windows in the living room.

As soon as he opened the window, the sound of hundreds of screaming girls poured into the firehouse. On a daily basis, girls surrounded the Lucas home, patiently waiting for just one peek at the band. This caused serious problems for the boys and their family. They couldn't even go out to buy groceries without getting swarmed. But sometimes it had its upsides.

Bracing himself, Joe peeked his head out the window. The sound rose to a deafening roar. Putting his hands up to his mouth, Joe shouted, "Excuse me, girls! Anyone got a pen?"

As soon as the words left his mouth, a blizzard of pens came flying through the window. Joe ducked. Turning around, he saw the pens sticking out of the wall in a perfect heart-shaped pattern. Those girls had pretty good aim. Joe stood up and yelled out to them, "Thank you!"

Shutting the window, he walked over to the pens, pulled one out of the wall and sat down with his brothers to write a strongly worded letter to the editor.